经 典 照 亮 前 程

FORREST GANDER

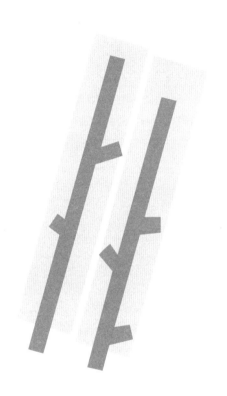

[美]弗罗斯特·甘德 著 李 栋 译

TWICE ALIVE

新生

华东师范大学出版社
·上海·

图书在版编目（CIP）数据

新生 /（美）弗罗斯特·甘德著；李栋译. —— 上海：华东师范大学出版社，2022
ISBN 978-7-5760-2449-4

Ⅰ.①新… Ⅱ.①弗…②李… Ⅲ.①诗集 – 美国 – 现代 Ⅳ.① I712.245

中国版本图书馆 CIP 数据核字 (2022) 第 028558 号

上海市版权局著作权合同登记 图字：09-2021-585 号

新　生

著　　者	[美]弗罗斯特·甘德	门市（邮购）电话	021-62869887
译　　者	李栋	门市地址	上海市中山北路 3663 号华东师
策划编辑	许　静		范大学校内先锋路口
责任编辑	乔　健	网　店	http://hdsdcbs.tmall.com
审读编辑	陈　斌		
责任校对	时东明	印刷者	上海中华商务联合印刷有限公司
装帧设计	卢晓红 郝钰	开　本	850×1168 32 开
封面插图	Rodrigo Corral	印　张	5.25
摄影插图	弗罗斯特·甘德	字　数	176 千字
		版　次	2022 年 8 月第 1 版
出版发行	华东师范大学出版社	印　次	2022 年 8 月第 1 次
社　　址	上海市中山北路 3663 号	书　号	ISBN 978-7-5760-2449-4
邮　　编	200062	定　价	65.00 元
网　　址	www.ecnupress.com.cn		
电　　话	021-60821666	出 版 人	王　焰
行政传真	021-62572105		
客服电话	021-62865537		

（如发现本版图书有印订质量问题，请寄回本社
客服中心调换或电话 021-62865537 联系）

弗罗斯特·甘德

我出生在莫哈韦沙漠。我去过也写过很多别的沙漠，如利比亚的撒哈拉、中国的戈壁、智利的阿塔卡马、美国的索诺拉、印度的塔尔等。像空白的一页，沙漠让我彻底谦卑。我所做的一切都不能让沙漠或是文学那一页变得更好。

我和一位伟大的诗人 C. D. 莱特一起生活了三十多年。她是我见过的最具美德、慷慨、诚实、热心的人。我们在物质世界里的感官生活和书本里的精神世界不可分割。

我成年的大部分时间里都对翻译着迷。即使在小时候，我的阅读也很国际化；翻译过来的童话和神话培养了我的想象力。

中国的古典诗词对我的影响巨大。近二十年来，我有幸推介过一批中国当代诗人的作品。我（跟人）合译过日本诗人吉增刚造和野村喜和夫的作品，还译介过许多拉丁美洲和西班牙诗人，尤其是西班牙语女诗人的作品。

我一直对和其他领域的艺术家合作有兴趣，如电影、摄影、陶艺和雕塑等。我觉得这种合作就是我所希望的开放敏感地生存在这世上的方式。

献给阿诗维妮·芭特和拉克希密·芭特

没有地衣的花园 / 是没有希望的花园
—— 德鲁·米尔恩

生命的每一刻 / 我都活过 / 第二次……
—— 朱塞培·翁加雷蒂

谁需要去害怕融合？
—— 沃尔特·惠特曼

目录

CONTENTS

新生

亲密关系的生态

作者前言

我们许多人在高中时代学到的关于地衣的知识——说它是污染的指示生物（石蕊实际上来自地衣）；还说它是真菌和藻类或蓝细菌的协同联盟——这些说法虽然在很大程度上都是正确的，但也过于简单化了。如果地衣生态更多的是合作而不是竞争关系，那么这样的合作是具有革命性意义的。相对于植物而言，地衣可能与动物的关系更密切。原来的生物体在结合中被彻底改变且无法复原。根据当代著名真菌学家安妮·普林格尔的说法（我曾有幸与她合作），若能提供足够的养分，地衣可能不会衰老。安妮和其他当代生物学家都认为，我们对死亡不可避免的这种认识可能是由我们哺乳动物的生命形式而决定的。也许有些生命形式具有"理论上的不朽性"。地衣可以进行无性繁殖，在此过程中，繁殖双方的一部分会在一块新的表面融合。那么，一个血统的繁殖双方可以繁衍多久？这个没有人知道。两个个体融合、相互改变和作用而形成不会衰老的新个体，这让我联想到亲密关系的本质。在最为亲密的关系中，我们不是经常意识到自己的身份以及所有的身份都可以相融组合吗？

晨曲

你能否听到黎明慢慢靠近，听到　·　柔和的光和它真空的
指尖　·　扣住卧室的墙壁，一句轻描淡写的　·　什么？
是欣喜？你能否听到那些声音，　·　如果可以叫声音的话，
那些红眼雀　·　在院子里抓挠着，然后是　·　咯吱、低沉、
沙哑的　·　声音在你床边裹着点点睡意　·　娓娓道来
说着一个梦，仿佛就在眼前，　·　而此刻，梦被打断了，
你能否　·　听出那个声音，如果可以　·　叫声音的话，虚无
开了口　·　和你亲昵地说着，就这样直接，我知道　·　你一定
会听出情绪，一阵低低的震颤打在　·　你的骨头里，难道你
不觉得自己　·　已迷失在给你的一生之外的下一个瞬间吗？

靠我们自己

即使意识到我们已停滞，在每一个
最基本的方面都停滞不前，此时
我们看到自己在下坠，甚至会
更加紧紧地受制于脑海中的漩涡，
意象在眼前飞驰，一条蓝鲸
在波利纳斯海滩上腐烂，恶臭
向南飘去，那里有数十头身长四十英尺
嵌满藤壶的灰鲸，死于饥饿，残骸
拍打着海岸，波浪泛白的
额头冲击着那些
山丘般大小的油腻的烂肉，一眼
望去，满眼都是这样，要是有心看的话，
我们就着一口就能吞下的小方块奶酪
和森宝利葡萄酒，等一切
都成了月亮穹顶下的低吟，或是有心
去听一簇簇野生的稞麦
轻拂着沙丘，此时
碎石沿着断层线发出尖锐的声响
分贝低得只有指挥着地面声音的
脚底直到我们的距骨
才能记录下正在发生的

事件

就在那里，我们的生命

被割离成了别的什么，

被抽干了内涵，沉浸于自我的优越，

我们和那些所谓的朋友一起反抗，

而这些人近来似乎

迟步于我们的问候，

让我们怀疑

他们也感觉到了问题，

远离内心，这或许暗示着

深渊般的不快乐？凝神

在傍晚

像一头白色的、幽灵般的

黇鹿被引入岬角，

开始和当地的物种

竞争并胜出，

直到每一头都被雇佣的猎手

屠杀殆尽，掀起

关于什么才是本地物种的争论，

假定所有的生态系统都趋于变化。或许

我们的耳朵在抽搐。或许是鹿的耳朵

在抽搐。但在一片昏暗中

我们仍然无法看清

我们在看的是什么，还是可以看清？

喧嚣迎面而来，没有间歇，
需要咀嚼的琐事，手机的叮叮声
渴望得到即时的回复，纯粹
过于丰盛的、现时的
耻辱塞满了每一分钟
从而代替了活出自己的
所有意义，每一个举手投足
都成了一场表演，我们想象的
观众永远都不会停滞，
永远都会看着我们。而萌发出的
所谓的激情呢？或是感性的
瞬间融入了我们的步子，
我们感觉到了什么，
我们的影子合在了一起（不是
浪漫，而是我们相依相存的
真实结果），我们与
险峻的峡谷里针叶树的影子
合在了一切，完全赤裸，
没有救赎，世界把我们解析成了
非人性的事物，而簇生的
地衣在岩石上泛起了波澜，不缺少
什么来为我们的存在
作出回应？
而现在，我们中的一些人

被经济现实所打败，

躺在多洛雷斯公园，像掉落的果实

等待着腐烂。还有一些人发现自己

接受了一种微不足道、自圆其说的善意。

吐出海藻的珊瑚、隐退的繁星、

苏醒的苔原又如何？我们相互思量着

怎能忍受，即使是自己遗憾举动的

分量？生命，有人反驳说，

是纯粹的、自由生发的广阔境界。就睁眼

去看吧：光在那儿，那是恩典本身。但

此刻已近晌午，一眼望去，

山丘开始泛起白光，

在可见的范围内，环绕在我们身边的，

我们默默感到，是退潮的时光。

新生

地衣共生菌刚开始**包围**
共生光合物，两者皆蜕变
成其他事物，自己的生命
和有争议的相互性，新生，
海藻细胞**被束缚**在簇群中

你用三镜头的珠宝寸镜来检查
脐带地衣、磐石地衣的**附着根**，
接着是爱好和平的鹅膏菌
蜂拥周围的是一种没有肛门的螨虫
然后是美味的鸡油菌，别名叫死亡号角

干旱时的极度喑哑

让地衣继续生存下去
露水与雾气一样的
零星事件，**天鹅绒般**的
绒毛和潮湿的皮层

我用拇指在手指间揉碎橡树苔，
让它的甜**香**在我抚摸你的喉咙时
一直留在你的皮肤上，香气久久地
不散去，让人回忆起在砂岩悬崖上
看到**旭日**地衣

尽管壳状地衣喜欢
腐烂，但**流浪**地衣都具有
吸湿性，孢子喷出
在入侵的前线
薄壁**开裂**

如果食草动物吃了**狼**地衣，它们
就会死亡，食肉动物吃了狼地衣，
它们就会在痛苦中**痉挛**而死，唯一的
例外是老鼠，而地衣的生死
却几乎不能分辨出来

食地衣的螨虫
干裂**粪便**扬起的纤维
引发了樵夫湿疹，
伐木工人的祸害，
深陷锯雪松时的**甜**蕨中

有水的情况下，共生光合物会膨胀
光合作用的生物体会变得僵硬
数小时在黑暗中呼吸，精液般的**嫩玉米**气味
变成了片状蘑菇的形态

在空化的共质体中，孢子松动
进入**伸长**区，潜鸟呜咽的夜晚

傍晚时分，我们来到这片森林的边缘，
在一棵枯死的橡树下
根腐菌**闪闪发亮**，树发光的
根茎反射在一只觅食的浣熊眼里，
不过，它还没有发现我们

潮湿的空气幽灵般地跟着
我们从树林里走出来
望着田野那边第一条
房子亮着灯的小道，它暗淡的
锡金的光环被湿湿的雾气盖住

冬虫夏草——你褐色的眼睛在雨水中
变得柔和，远看带着**荧光** ——几天后
消融成了**黏液**，无论我们认为我们
所跟着的是什么，它都跟着我们，它
的意图与我们的无关

桑格姆声学

森林

橡树的情欲区间

        悬挂着

               花边地衣的披肩

太阳的光辉洒落

        树叶间

               一片斑驳一种力量

称它为夜色吧

        把蘑菇推出

               它们的巢穴

菌丝体

        壤土中一股港口的味道

               它们突然出现

在自由自在的空气中

　　　带着深吸的一口气

　　　　　伴随着胸前微动

它们像记忆？或是标点？是

　　　　　大地说的什么

　　　　　　　来唤起我们的回应

要求我们回忆起

　　　　我们过去的历史中

　　　　　　进化的历程

带我们成为

　　　　大众中的

　　　　　一员

和内心中的

　　　　新生的孩子注意到我的爱人

　　　　　　你突然出现在我的身边了吗

还是你从一开始就在这里

　　　　　一股子的意义和腐朽

　　　　　　　　　仍紧紧抓住地下世界

我们两个人半埋在地下，坚守着

　　　　　即使仅仅是短暂的膨胀

　　　　　　　　　到浩瀚星空我们的结合开始

被记录在

　　　　　已警醒的汇编中

　　　　　　　　包围我们而你包围着我

一种盛大淹没了我们

　　　　　将我们冲开整整一个上午

　　　　　　　　　我们充盈着对方

就像头顶的鸟鸣般破碎

　　　　　谁升上了表面

　　　　　　　　让我们的面容跃起

流浪海洋

她的不可接近唤起了他的欲望，他渴望
在他的身体里活着更多她的生命。看着

     破碎的浪花，站得如此地近，他可以感觉到
      她湿漉漉的头上散发的热。他和

眼前这个人是什么关系
在他面前的这个人，既熟悉又陌生？他

     在她脸上搜寻着的其实是他自己。一阵阵的风
      吹动浪的尖头，春草旋转着

在沙地上打着圈，他们站着不说话。她
想让他知道一切都包含情感，即使是草

     和花粉也是正负两极，所以当草舞动起来，

就会在空中拂过花粉。他感到周围都带着电

仿佛即将来临的风暴要上演的狂野戏剧
已经注意到了他们，这两个岸上的外国人。小小的

蓝宝石般的花儿点缀着沙丘。
他想知道是不是他让自己被打平

变成没有深度的薄片，就像自动扶梯，最后他是否
会消失在地下，没有最微小的

阻力。但当她那张奢华的脸转向他
微笑，她的眼角被风吹湿了，

他屈服于这种过度，他重新出现在自己面前。

在山中

> "没有外部的身体。更好的说法是，
> 外部发生在身体内部"
> ——胡安·塞巴斯蒂安·卡德纳斯

如果四月的无精打采在你的信之前被她收到

如果你后门口沾满螨虫的蘑菇变成了啮齿动物的颜色

那么她的大腿会颤抖，站起身的时候，她的头会变轻

如果她的虹膜发光，如果你发黑的面庞从她的瞳孔中回望，如法
院传票般枯燥

那么你必须承认你已被刺穿的预兆

如果你再吸一口尘土，记住该说的话

如果她称之为你的悲伤的淤泥不再阻塞你的血管

她能瞥见你转向自我内心前的情境吗？

如果遗憾在你身后喋喋不休地出现

那么她会蒙住你的眼睛说：尝一口吧

如果只需要再划掉一个名字就能结束悲哀

如果山上传来的哀声在她脸上得到了回应

当她躺在你的身上，你的喘气声听起来像戏剧中的废话

如果你总会选择思考前的第一反应

那么她会喊道"哦，不"，仿佛惊讶她不能自已

如果西高止山脉吞下一个碳化的太阳

如果她把你眼角的一闪误以为是一个信号

如果她把篮子放在厨台上，篮子上最熟的芒果滚了下来

你必须忘记拉开她长袍的另一双手

如果当地的动物为了躲避你而在夜里活动，如果成群的笑鸫不再从山顶上飞下

那么她的眼睛在黑夜里发出的最微弱的光会吸引你

可是如果这橙色的地衣——在巨石上闲聊似的扩散——发黑了，卷了起来，沉默了？

田园

雨突然停了　　　在一小时以前，转弯
转弯信号灯停止了　　　最后的咯吱声，而

我们抵达了　　　抵达一座废弃的农场
还有其他人此刻　　　把自己解脱出来

下了车，我们的声音　　　掺和了
轻松，还有　　　兴奋，某种

幸福的冒险，如果　　　可以这么说的话，而这
并非假装：大笑、摔　　　车门，易混合的我们相信

我们是朋友，记得吗?　　　你那些鲜花般的
伴娘还戴着　　　　　　　紫色的鸡蛋花头巾

像果阿邦的嬉皮。蜿蜒曲折　　　通往河流的路散发蒸汽——
在日光下蒸腾　　　使一切更充盈却没有

增加重量。你，　　　这个地方对你而言是熟悉的，
甚至是神圣的，所以并没有　　　给你什么，你指着

泥地上孔雀留下的足迹。穿过　　一座老果园，在我们
身旁，肿胀的菠萝蜜　　挂在纤细的枝条上，

成群的蠓虫　　上下晃动着
像是清风中的发　　网。还没

看清，我们已听到　　河水的水声
以及再往后面　　潺潺的径流
冲下捣实的冲积层断崖　　蓝花楹香水
混合着来自你邻居　　养殖场的

异味。谁能看着　　那个下午直至
尾声？我们整个　　队伍停了下来，你

单膝跪地，你蹲下　　在水坑边
向一只肥硕的蟾蜍发出咕咕声。大家　　沉默了

我们被你脸上　　标志性的热情
给迷住了。太阳　　抚开白云，你

回眸瞥见了我的眼睛　　附在你身上的眼睛
我那时的感觉　　让我有理由

回忆起　　音乐家脸上

绽放的喜悦　　　在最后音符的

停顿间　　　最后的音符和掌声的
停顿间。你　　　说的，我说的。我们

做的事会一直做到我们之间没有了间隙。

荒芜之地（给圣罗莎）

绿色的春草

　　　在山丘上枯死

　　　　　那是六月，到了七月

　　　　　　　　　　枯草变得毛茸茸

　　　　　　　变成了褐色，草噼啪地响

　　　　　在脚下，干巴巴的

在活着的橡树的

　　　一片喧嚣中，被感染

　　　　　小幼虫附着

　　　　　　　　　　在下侧腹叶上

　　　　　　　在叶脉间

　　　　　进食。蛀屑，

即粪便的细屑

　　　　和无聊的粉尘，丁零着

　　　　　　　落到树枝下

　　　　　　　　　　　枯死的叶子上。你
　　　　　　　在二十英尺开外
　　　　　能听到丁零声。

山谷的另一头，

　　　　在塔糖山岭上，

　　　　　　　一轮满月冒出了头

　　　　　　　　　　像是一位少女在翻筋斗。
　　　　　　　没有人可以在不存在的人生里
　　　　　生活下去。

烟雾、热浪、火焰和风

　　　形成的巨柱下，

　　　　　我起身，颤巍巍地

　　　　　　在紊乱的大脑漩涡中摇晃，

　　　　即兴发挥着我自己的

极端天气，吸入

数亩烧焦的

　　表土，像一阵燃烧的冻雨

　　　　向外旋转

　　　　　　　和着污物和灰烬

　　　　　我被向前推进

　　　我的嘴一直张开

朝着每一个方向。所以

　　　　我为你而来，汹涌澎湃

　　　　　　当下变成了炼狱

　　　　　　　　　　　　　　因为我需要

　　　　　　　　在我能看清前

　　　　　把一切都变成悲剧，因为

必须

　　掺杂着悔恨

　　　　这种感觉才能升华。

晨曲 二

给奥茨

从他自己的肩上 · 拔出箭杆 · 在山的
东脊上 · 带一把纯铜的斧头 · 和未消化的山羊
肉 · 针叶树花粉，晚来的春天 · 熊皮雪地靴 · 小
袋子装着生火的工具 · 燧石碎片和一只木蹄层孔菌 ·
数小时来蘑菇温暖着余烬的火花 · 他头昏脑涨地倒下
摔在了肚子上 · 冻了融了又冻了 · 就这么五千年 ·
在痛苦之外 · 他听到了什么，光闪烁着 · 闪
在山的脸庞上 · 什么通过耳朵进入了他的身体 ·
通过他荒凉、惶恐、恍然的眼睛 · 他拿走了的
东西 · 他说不出名字

靠我们自己 二：散落世界的持续存在

在盛夏的沥青热浪中

冷杉在一片巨大碎屑流旁边颤抖着

就你知我知，向导俯身向前

放低声音说，你必须

不再期望自己可以

把所有的事情都处理好

在酷儿的时代，说这话很酷儿

我们说，我们使用中性代名词

她回答说，有谁会

认为任何人都只是单一性的个体？

我们回来的时候，朋友们都很紧张

你们看到盖丘亚蜂鸟了吗？

你们看到委内瑞拉蜂鸟了吗？

采花蜂鸟和紫薇蜂鸟那儿也有吗？

在墙的另一头？

那纳瓦特尔小蜂鸟呢？

不要说，它飞到你面前快速扇动翅膀的时候

你眨了眼，向导说

别乱说，你看到太阳蜂鸟了吗？

我们承认在佩塔卢马曾见过蜂鸟花

一只从墨西哥向北飞来的大蓝喉蜂鸟

但玛雅蜂鸟逃得太快了

好像知道我们会对它的花园做什么

被冬雨唤醒的蓝藻出鞘丝状体

在土壤中蜿蜒而行

在傍晚留下长而黏的痕迹

我们站在自家的门廊上欣赏着

月光下事物柔和的轮廓就好像

我们身处里希特的画中，或是

某个广告宣传中诱人的图像间

在一池化学物质中生发

去恢复生命本身的游戏，是啊

是啊，当然是，我们现在说是！

我们曾试着去体谅别人

但这他妈的就是一场骗局

危险品运输车像青蛙一样

在达到目的地时发出哗哗声

尽管谁会注意到

他们的眼睛都盯着新的电视节目

记者没有说火番茄，他说的是

火龙卷，用一只眼看深渊

是否这区别无足轻重

就像我是多样的和一定要喜欢我，

或其他我们相互劝慰的建议，

让无法承受的变得可以承受？

我们的花蜜仍然吸引着昆虫

尽管我们已喷洒了草甘膦

蜘蛛似的贝斯手一直待在舞台的角落

沉默把一个世界联系到另一个世界

开花的一面总会感染畸形

在争论间，我们注意到

彼此的对峙就像两个扭曲的空间

吞噬着从我们渐渐融合的洞中

发出的引力的尖叫

尽管我们承认一定程度的装腔作势

每个人都以为自己的才是肉食主菜

你在开玩笑吧。我无意间听到向导这么说，真的吗？

你就是这样生活的吗？所以

寂寞的夜晚就像一罐绿色油漆

被泼到餐车的窗子上，我们看着

长长的边境围墙飞速驶过

列车员录音说，请好好利用你的盐分时间

因为你已深陷痛苦之中

新生 二：太浩国家森林

如果那是一团黑色的胶质菌

在腐烂的松枝上，如果那是一个拇指长

半透明卵囊，在白蚁皇后身后**跳动**

如果旭日穿过百叶窗，将我们一起唤醒，

或者是在明天，如果**橙黄银耳**可以学会说话

长而柔软、纱笼般的**苔藓**

迷倒了岩石、树桩、向上

翘起的花岗岩和片麻岩

松针、黑莓、荆棘

湿漉漉的，**杂乱**地拱起

我们走下灌木丛山坡

我们的呼吸在轻浮的早晨
清晰可见，我们进入颤巍巍的
杨树林，**海绵般松软**的地面
小道两旁浮起涟漪
有乳白色的可食用羊肚菌

还有有毒的**假**羊肚菌，我们的
气息下是苔藓的歌声，你走之前
你说，<u>不要那么理性，电子产品
是理性的</u>，我在想我要做出怎样的
改变，我的下一句话才不至于如此

之后你的小黑蚊子·电报让我整晚都无法
入眠，在长廊上在能看到它们之前
我可以听到大**飞蛾**的声音，最后我躺在
你的**缺失**留给我的巨大空间，猫抓了抓

我的前胸，你酸臭的浴巾模糊了我的脸

我被折磨了一天，一会儿就抽鼻子，
高粱般厚实的鼻涕不断，其实我也是
从某些纠缠在一起的菌丝体中暂时升起的
血肉之躯的突起物，所以我说话的时候，
逝者也说话，**哦**，神圣又神圣的交融

之后就是身体慢慢**疲倦**
之后是那只棕色的白嘴鸽子
平平地贴在了沙子上，某种力量
在我们能命名之前就代我们表达了
雪松树上飘来的香气**淹没**了一切

桑格姆声学 二

大火后的森林

阴影重叠着阴影，没有了树冠，
碳化了的树木枝干排成一个个
方阵，内部的动量早已短路。
清晨，它们缠绕着我们
像地质深成的柱子，像失语的先知
领读着感恩祭中的颂谢词，像某次
漫长屠戮的残留物。唯一在浮动的
是升起的雾气，模糊得都称不上
幽灵一般，弥散在雨打湿的土地
被烧焦的菌丝状土层的上空。森林中
所剩下的，在感叹的语气中
继续。在一种语言里，表达
燃烧成灰烬，一切微不足道的
都已挥发，对大火而言，
一切都微不足道。附近的
山丘上，黑色的痉挛拉碴一片，
从一处裂口，我们看到了
熟悉的太阳，那在吹气管口
形成球状的液体玻璃。如果这片景象
在做着它的梦，那它一定得梦醒自己。

所有人都察觉到，对幸福，
你有一种鲜有的天赋。我思量着
在遍地残骸间穿行，该如何看待。
第二天，一只背部黑色的
啄木鸟回应了你的呼唤，可我们
一直找到黄昏都没有找到它。

大海：在波利纳斯冲夜浪

或许有足够的光　·　能看到浪　·　映着月光、沙
　·　映着月光和你　·　在岸上远远望着　·　你
看到的　·　仅仅是破浪的身影　·　白蓝交接
浪花蒸腾起泡　·　当浪尖坠落　·　冲天般爆破
　·　底浪穿过　·　一刹那间的清晰快速　·　被
夜色掩盖　·　浪冲得唑唑作响、汹涌澎湃　·
汇入黑暗之中　·　剧烈的鼾声　·　与之竞争的
没有别的声音

在危险的逆流中划行　·　齐腰高的西北海浪　·
断裂区　·　如同进入一堵黑曜石墙　·　与夜空
无异　·　潜入水下，快速划行　·　坐下之前　·
一只手臂放在冲浪板上　·　我急速蹲下　·　在
水下听一刻　·　外来的音符　·　不是白天引擎
声呐的咔嚓、呜咽声　·　而是低频的嗡嗡声　·
是鱼、乌贼、甲壳动物　·　集体上游觅食特有的
声音，我感到　·　一种阴森的平和，恐惧缠绕

二十分钟后，眼睛　·　适应了，手划开水面　·

后面留下生物光的痕迹 · 没有足够的光 · 来
发现近处的疖子 · 或缺陷 · 浪头显得更大了 ·
快速逼近 · 之后是五次短促的划水进入 · 无维度的
剥离器 · 两个 S 形转向 · 出围上岸 · 你的叫喊

怯懦使我的目光 · 从空荡荡的海滩上移开 ·
和你在一起我意识到 · 一种特有的契机 · 尽管
我并不相信 · 客观的描述，有的只是 · 混乱、经验、
感知 · 时而分享的世界 · 尽管生命并不被分享 ·
承受，有的只是 · 持续的空 · 但你的活力搅动了它
· 留下兴奋的痕迹 · 我已经从自我的谷底 · 升起
并发现 · 我存在于你 · 存在于我 · 在困境中，我甚至
体会到了升华 · 罕见的事件 · 而需要的 · 只是一个证人

在山中，普莱瑟县

……谁钝滞的手指，角闪石指甲被剪掉，
绕着（如此轻盈地穿过缝隙的纽扣）

和她的绿色喜悦的蛇形
笑声回荡在中央的山谷（他们的电车俯冲）

车门在她身后被重重地关上，她面对着
牛仔裤裂口的圆形剧场（一直到她的私处）

他注视的双眼里筑巢的愉悦在她眼里
没有半点缝隙（她的双眼也注视着）

他面庞的使命之外，他们像教堂的钟一样
在摇摆（物质总是向外晃动的）

温暖的焦糖美分的味道（哦不要，
哦不要）在受冰川漂砾律动下的湿度

她驱车上坡，他问她在哪里、什么时候
学会这么开？（飞速下坡）

一条响尾蛇绕起了圈（她的躯干在臀部之上）
她在一连串的冰碛石上留下了颤动的痕迹

（一双黑暗的太阳）光环扩大
吸力的漩涡沿着融化的溪流旋动

当祈求者慢慢弯腰，长长的
大腿沿着关节面分开

没有疑虑的暗流，每一部分都欣然向往，森林
侵袭着灰暗的大地（她的膝盖开始抽搐）

田园

一起，
你
站在
我的面前，在
大落地窗的
前面，我的双臂
环抱着你，我们的
眼睛投射在
我们的身影之外，进入——

（"进入"，我这么写
好像在那里
投向隧道的
尽头，
一条点缀着
无尽的
目的
之地，就
好像我们的目光
刚刚在脸庞之外
开始

并以螺旋的方式

向地平线延伸，

过程式的，

就好像看

需要时间才能发生

而不是

瞬间即时的，

整个儿

一笔给出，

我们

问之前，在意志

之前，好像远处的

索诺玛山脉

并不像我们

那样已准备好

被看成

窗台上

死去的苍蝇）——

远处，一座

广阔的山丘

鲜艳的芥末

在晨光的照耀下

被诱开了花

荒芜之地

你将永远后悔对她做出的心胸狭窄的
小残忍，

                 没有开花的楝树、环切虫、
                          掩土的

甲虫、黄黑相间的苹果蛀虫
和它令人作呕的臭味

          在你分心的时候，这些虫子在花园里大肆
                   破坏。就在

她领你走出什么的时候。
一种苦楚里的另一种苦楚，

             你每晚都把她拉回来，直到你们之间
                什么都没有留下

只剩下对衰老的恐惧
和你不知疲倦的

自我关注。那晚，也就是你所谓

回来的

最后那晚，她给你
发了消息。

宝贝，我想你，想象一下

你坐在皮转椅上，

穿着丝绸内裤，我把衣服掀开一点

坐在你身上（你不会有问题

滑入我的身体），我背对着你，你的手

在我袖子里

抬头一看，地平线已经变成了

　　　　　红色，好像一根透明的动脉，而在你下面

一条鳄鱼蜥蜴继续

　　　　　在长谷火山臼

温暖的灰烬上下滑

　　　　　在有毒的烟雾中去挖她的窝。这些年

你的脚步把一条磨损的道路

　　　　　咀嚼成了地衣寻找

边缘的凝灰岩。你已经失去了

　　　　　嗓音的抑扬顿挫。没有人需要

告诉你这些。她的缺失

　　　　　一次又一次地

像暗井穿过摇摇欲坠的基岩

　　　　　　　　　　　　穿过你。没有

什么会一如既往

　　　　　　　　　　　　除了蚂蚁的集会

晨曲 三

我们管理着富人的游泳池　·　我们为狗打开
副驾驶的门　·　在皮卡里等着的狗　·　盯着
餐厅入口的狗　·　当我们出来，拿着用纸巾
包着的一大卷墨西哥卷饼时　·　兴奋的呜咽声
　·　我们不　·　感到完全孤单　·　尽管事实
如此　·　我，所有之中最坏　·　在阿里昂的打印机，
弄湿亚麻布　·　这样打出来的字会投下阴影　·　之后
在傍晚　·　把铅字都扔回　·　到废铅字箱　·　我们
试着用镜子　·　去治疗一个幽灵般的肢体　·　但
缺失的　·　其实在我们内心　·　有些人在黎明
登机前　·　乱扔帮派标识，抽着大麻　·　永远
坐在飞机跑道上　·　猛吸前面飞机烧掉的燃料　·
头顶的管道喷出毒气　·　反射在灰暗的窗子上　·
我们自己的眼睛朝后看　·　眼前一片空白　·　这时
中微子从我们身上穿过

靠我们自己 三：看清事物

看清事物而不是习惯已经
熟悉的模式——一个未被预料到的
整体就在那里，投下一对阴影，操纵
它的材料、推进、组装出足够多的
我们称之为生命的亲缘关系，我们的生命，
其实已经是许许多多的生命了，它的规模
在我们生活期间被笼罩了一层面纱——

穿过相邻细胞的细胞质
一个信号让你转向我，让我
进入你。我们在安静的骚动中
结合在一起，趋同的争论、陌生的
节奏变得熟悉。一种节奏是
我在这里，永远不会被剥去。
我们成为一个东西

　　　　　　　　　　倾听

什么存在，什么不存在。在风暴中，
山上的楝树在它们的根部

疯狂地跺脚。我们已经走过了
春天，但什么东西又走过了
我们？现在，你的笑声
使我透明化。而谁的
自我意识不发生变化？你无条件的
外来性变得有条件了，不再
是外来的了。你在我身旁，
我对世界的视角也随之改变。一阵
蠕动式的收缩以一个波浪的形式

穿过我们。我们不再能保持距离。
我们的嘴唇，或者说我们的一角，擦过对方。

但你对我轻声低语的是什么语言，
你的牙齿被尼尔吉里茶染红，
在高处的颤音和口哨声中，在推土机
把瓦砾推向受伤的街道的尖叫声中，
在无眼的虱子爬上草茎的沉默声中？我什么
也不明白，只知道你的声音煽动的欲望，
宣泄的柔情。怎样、谁又能说清楚
是什么力量在这一时刻让我们
小小的声音融合成一种这之前

并不存在的肉欲？

来到这个未曾预料到的
结合点，我们滑入
彼此，在热的脉搏中
抓紧对方，在是与否之间，
因为我们已经可以看清
我们已经不再是从前的我们

我发现你在我的身体里——不是融合，
不是联结，而是筑巢一般。对你而言，
也是这样吗？——投入的
力度，我们兴奋于
对方的波动

匆匆推动就好像有什么——
或许是我们的嘴唇相擦而过或者
是我们自身的一角——剥离了
什么？——之前是什么？之前
真的有什么吗？

重组是瞬间即逝的

体验。它就是<u>自我的</u>

<u>存在</u>。但现在是谁的存在？我是否

被赋予了某种特殊的柔韧度，

成为了你的一部分，却没有

经历自我的消亡？那么

之前的你的逝去对我意味着什么，

尽管现在的你在我面前，一直如此。

因为过量过度才能

使我们转变，让我们燃烧。你的

生命超越了自身。难道你不能

在欣喜若狂的开放中感受到我吗？

就像下的雨和红色的泥土混合到了一起。

没有你，我活了过来。有了你，

我再次在激进的身份扩大中

活了过来。因为我们已经

突破了自身的外部极限，因为

我们召唤了对方。在你身上，

我的生命超越了自身。

新生 三：
步行环绕塔玛佩斯山

斑驳的光从树冠的孔隙
失重坠落，我们的感官
属于周围**轮回**的生命，穿过
灌木丛，兴奋于**看不见的**事物
我们的脚步声回荡着

我们向上攀登，雾气中弥漫着
杰弗里松**奶油硬糖**的味道
直到我们到达一片蜻蜓的
荒地、一片**紫荆**花和开阔的天空，
低洼的芒草丛上一层白霜

在红木溪，两个
一起跑步的人穿过
一座木桥，跨过
我们前面的一条小溪
一只**西丛鸦**嘎吱嘎吱嘎吱地叫

坚持走完米尔谷的浸海径，
飞机缓缓的呻吟在海湾方向减弱，
汗水湿透了的体恤在我身上
变得清凉，又一位跑步者从我旁边
超过，他**翘起**的手臂举得太高

心脏山的花岗岩巨石好像
刚被修剪过。看，你说，
我可以看到费拉隆群岛
向南的长背山

一座连着一座，一只乌鸦**叫**了

在登上石头泉的路上，
月亮仍挂在道格拉斯
冷杉上空，黄蜂和小红蛱蝶
停留在小径上，某条地下的
细流滋润着土壤

我估计你会躲在月桂树荫下
啃你那
三条凤尾鱼配奶酪的
三明治，而我则平躺在巨石上
在**阳光**下，吮吸着一只梨

毛毛虫的粪便叮叮当当地落在橡树
底下的一床枯叶上，一只老鹰**停下**
被一群**愤怒**的乌鸦包围着，我们
痛苦于不知道将会发生什么，
世界向前冲去，作自我介绍

一簇簇小绿点、**苦涩**的牡蛎
排在你手上的黑棒上，孱弱的
树木靠向我们，就好像是
潮湿黑暗的一部分，在枯叶下
滋养着根，还有蜜环菌

由于蜜环菌从土壤中吸食
化学物质能引发树木的
防御机制，它们在**不被觉察**的
情况下榨取树木的汁液，

同时分泌毒素来阻止
竞争物种的入侵

但是在它们薄薄根丝的
不可分割的遗传**嵌合体**中
任何单一物种的身份
在相互交流的种群中
都是模糊的，**新**生

快到山顶时，闪闪发光的
滑擦面岩层的露头
让小径变得神圣，蜿蜒地
穿过**绿色片岩**的辖区
其**致命**的矿物质使地面贫瘠

某个大昆虫的嗡嗡声
伊麦尔曼式地在我们
头顶回旋，让我回想起
你跟我说过的佛教徒
低沉的诵经声

但我们怎么能听出是自己
无法解读的诵经声呢——别
这么理性——透红嫩枝的
集合语言，一种
导管的语言，发生在我们

呼吸的语言之前，肢体、化学的，
把我们的声音引入谐音，领我们
看还没有见过的事物，周遭的环境
呼唤着我们，毫无理论，沿着水平

线上结合的推断，就发生在

地平面上，一句咒语
独立（于我们）却能觉察到，**圆满**
总是（对我们）排斥却煽动
我们去认知在这里
可能的意义——在人类或非人类之间——

这里，在家里，我们的认知
是把我们带过去的又一个小小的声音，
带着我们，进入**无物相间**，
走出我们的视线，孕育孢子的嘴巴
道出一串连祷

菌丝伸**长脖子**
张开喉咙，打开
系统之间的联系
句法的过度饱和
一种**唤醒**，即使

高分贝声呐的
滚动墙震破鲸鱼的**耳朵**
即使大火无节制地燃烧
泥浆坑渗入小溪，等等
杀害女性、战争、所谓正义的

坚持，仍然坚持，
生命的触动**仍然**能
导入感觉中枢，难道
你听不到——别这么

理性——世界在吸气？——听到

别处的呼唤，也就是
我们所在的地方，不，甚至
更近，在我们体**内**，在我们
身体血液的脉搏中，我们
苔藓的绒毛，**拥抱**——，呼气

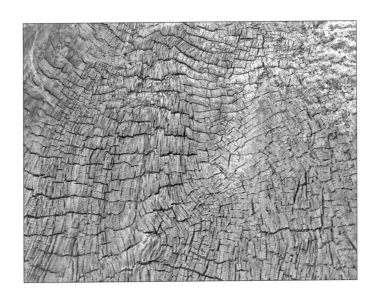

加州红木

．．．

——在近处，但在哪里？

/ \

在充满类萜的空气里在　　迭代的红木树枝间

\ / \

现在聚满了　　　附生植物的垫子

/ |

/ 一只暗冠蓝鸦开始了又开始

/ /

它被切碎的琶音——　　不是描述——还有

\ \

筑巢的海雀一只黑色柔情的　　眼睛反射

　　　　　　　／
田鼠的滑稽戏，　　　　　圆滚滚，长着胡须
　　　　　　\
圆柱状的绒毛认真地——这　　不是描述，而是
　　　　　　\　　　　　　／
不为人知的章节——　　　　在脸颊里
　　　　　　／
装满绿色的针叶

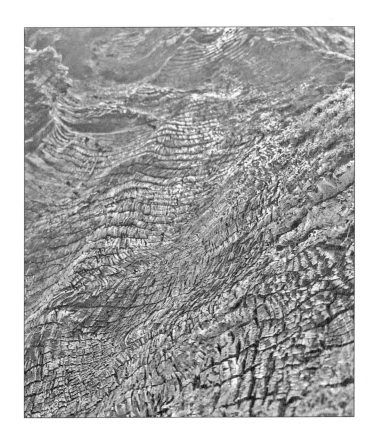

两百英尺以下，　　　　　　　　　　　　　植被下层，
　　　／　　　　　　　　　　　　　　　　　　／
鞭子藤被横枝、枯叶、酸模　　　　　　　　　刺穿
　｜　　　　　　　　　　　　　　　　／
还有剑和蕨菜　　　　　　从土壤中飞溅而出——不是
　　　＼　　　　　　　　　　　　　＼
描述，而是不　　　　　　为人知的章节，我们
　　　＼　　　　　　　　　　　　　／
自己的回忆录——满是　　　　　　张牙舞爪的火山岩，
　　　／　　　　　　　　　　　　　＼　　　／
主要是安山岩和白云岩，　　　　　还有腐烂的红木针叶
　　　＼　　　　　　　　　　　　　　　／
和谁能叫出名字的线虫动物和蜘蛛似的节足动物　　／
　　　　　　　　　　　　　　　　一起轻轻颤抖？

\
一只地松鼠，穿过 　　　干涸的小溪边
/ 　　　　　　　　　　　　 \　—
旁边是赤杨树，它的尾巴 　像旗杆一样笔直，它的
/ 　　　　　　　　　　　　　　 \
例子，所有的例子 　　　　相互渗透，
\ 　　　　　　　　　　　　　 /
一本无尽缠绕的回忆 　　　录，而我们的情况
\ 　　　　　　　　　　　　　 \
也一样得到了证实—— 　　　　　\
| 　　　　　　　　　　　　　　 /
在它的地道 　　　　　　　和大火在巨大的红木树干上
/ 　　　　　　　　　　　　　 /
烧出的洞之间乱窜， 　　　树干闪着鼻涕虫的痕迹，边缘
\ 　　　　　　　|
是正在生根的蘑菇

王红公的小屋

在前往 · 他小屋所在地的 · 路上，他的殿堂 · 从
另一种宗教抢夺 · 而来的殿堂 · 一种渔夫的宗教
 · 在拉古尼塔斯克里克 · 也就是魔鬼冲沟里的
拉古尼塔斯湖 · 进入森林的道路两旁 · 都被橙色、
黏稠的猴面 · 花所包围 · 无数粗壮、满是荷尔蒙的
 · 围栏蜥蜴在你面前 · 冲来撞去 · 像传令官似的
 · 你走在小径上 · 过了半英里 · 一只蓝舌石龙子，
它亮蓝色的尾巴直立在身后 · 斜着身子奔跑起来
越过小径然后 · 在满是蜘蛛网碎屑的 · 刺梅树下
消失不见了

印度的史诗文学 · 许多年前 · 他一直都在阅读，躺在
 · 这块灰岩板上 · 在欢快的溪流之上 · 他的头
藏在树荫下，他的 · 修长的身体很暖和 · 双腿
交叉着，太阳 · 枫叶的光芒透过 · 树木的枝叶
裹着苔藓 · 笨头笨脑地向外伸展着 · 向外伸出
冲沟 · 从一个陡峭的山坡上伸出 · 只有欧洲蕨类、
铁线蕨，还有 · 一对红刺黑毛虫的 · 放射状
绿色大爆炸 · 才能把山坡固定 · 虫子爬上他的皮靴 ·

在猖獗的琵琶树上，并肩在那儿 · 毛毛虫一直在
吞噬着 · 在所有印度的史诗文学中 · 提到的 ·
颜色不超过三种

看到了吗？他在这里，又不在这里。不 · 像你自己。
或者小溪中的水黾，在有节奏的收缩中划动 · 逆流
而上，你 · 站在岸边古树桩上的时候 · 在清澈
见底的水里看到了什么 · 昆虫的电鸣声 · 完美地
分布在整个树冠上 · 你在树下看到的 · 在透明的水
中 · 是一簇六个哥特式的黑影点 · 投射在河床上 ·
在那水黾单薄的、沙色的 · 身体下面 · 它们弓着身子
 · 在溪流的张力表面之上 · 不为人所见

不是这里。还有这里。尽管你 · 你已经徒步走过
森林中的土路 · 就像你出生之前他所做的那样 · 来到熟悉的地
方，两个不大瀑布的 · 汇流下 · 是
地面实况 · 他打鼾的小空地 · 煎两个鸡蛋当早餐
 · 盘腿坐在石板上随意涂鸦 · 进入

有你在其中的未来 · 你仍然在抵达 · 仍在 ·
抵达 · 没有小屋留下的痕迹，然而 · 他的存在
是不 · 可以分解的，你的思想 · 与不是你的 ·
思想融合在了一起，你的幸福 · 耀眼，你蹲着 ·
在存在与不存在的有形密度中倾听 · 而你成为了
你的 · 影子，与树影无间相邻

桑格姆声学：时间、空间和人类自我的融合

N. 马努·查克拉瓦西 [1]

　　森林、田园、海洋、山脉、荒地。桑格姆文学的主要景观也是加州的原始景观，即我的出生地和家园。我写的"桑格姆声学"诗受到印度和加州的经历以及桑格姆译诗的影响。桑格姆诗都暗指这五种地貌形态之一。即使原作被赞美，其文化影响也是复杂的。由于桑格姆诗学在美国鲜为人知，我邀请了学者查克拉瓦西为桑格姆诗学提供一些文学背景。

　　　　　　　　　　　　　　　　——弗罗斯特·甘德

　　"桑格姆"指的是一群拥有共同志向的人，他们在精神团结的基础上一起寻求形而上的意义与目的。正是"团结"这一因素，引导并滋养着这一群体。必须指出的是，共同的追求并不排除这一群体中的个别差异与分歧。趋同和等级与真正的桑格姆格格不入。群体中个体的眼光只会增强桑格姆的精神力量。

　　桑格姆的表述植根于耆那教和佛教的宗教哲学传统，其精髓体现在佛教的唱颂词中："Buddham Sharanam Gacchami,

---

1 N. 马努·查克拉瓦西（N. Manu Chakravarthy），杰出的文学评论家、印度国家电影奖年度最佳评论家、班加罗尔NMKRV女子学院英语教授。他在文学、音乐、女权主义、政治和电影方面著述颇丰。

Sangam Sharanam Gacchami, Dhammam Sharanam Gacchami"，意思是"我皈依佛陀，我皈依僧团，我皈依佛法"。这一颂词说明了要通过"僧团"（桑格姆）和遵守"佛法"的原则来寻求佛陀。把所寻求的事物转化为现实，既是深刻的个人经验，从某种意义上说也是集体的经验。

古典泰米尔文学被认为是"桑格姆文学"，从公元前300年至公元300年之间发展流传。关于桑格姆所持续的时间有很多种说法，有些夸张得像是神话般的叙述。然而，桑格姆这个词似乎确实是从耆那教和佛教进入古典泰米尔文学的。

学者们普遍认为有三个桑格姆时期，而第一时期的桑格姆文本没有被保存下来。据称，名为《托尔凯比安》（Tolkappiyam）的语法和修辞学文本属于第二时期。第三时期的桑格姆包括各种关于爱情的歌词，收录在一本名为《短集合》（Kuruntokai）的文集里。泰米尔诗根据主题被分为阿甘（Akam）和普拉姆（Puram）。

阿甘诗专注于内在，而普拉姆诗则关注外部公共空间。阿甘诗基本上是爱情诗，涉及人物的不同存在与情感状态，而普拉姆诗则关注战争、国王和英雄的荣耀以及道德价值观。普拉姆诗都交代了社会历史背景，并以现实世界为基础。从严格意义上讲，阿甘诗不具有历史性或特定的现实性，然而这并不意味着这些诗不具有现实意义。阿甘诗是关于现实世界和自然元素是如何在诗歌人物的经验状态中全然得以体现的。自然及其所包括的元素，如猫头鹰、山脉、鸟类、动物、贫瘠的土地、森林、季节，与个人的"内在景观"交相呼应。由此推之，鸟类、野兽和自然力量被有意识地转移到远远超出其原始栖息地的"异地",记录并强调了人物的情绪变化。"事物的自然秩序"的移位或错位是桑格姆诗歌的独特之处。换句话说,"外部"恰恰与观者相关联,即通过由渴望、渴求、结合、满足、分离、妄想、背叛等状态产生的各种情感。"自然"是人类思想对其作出的理解。正因为如此,自然物的特定身份会发生巨大变化,以此来记录与人物相关的全然不同的经验身份与实质。自然元素令人叹为观止的纵横交错是人类意识所承载的内在景观的一个重要标志,它改变了外部自然,使之与自己的形式和脾气相匹配。此外,自然以其各种形式存在,所有的基本品质都完好无缺,但在桑格姆诗歌中,"自然"超越了自身,"成为"心灵的隐喻。桑格姆诗歌中自然的蜕变本质上是外部景观的内化,消解了强烈的个体体验和所谓的不为外界所动的物质现实精神之间的对立和分离。"自然"与人类精神是一致的。

弗罗斯特·甘德的"桑格姆声学"在最高意义上讲是桑格姆意识的开花结果。甘德的诗歌属于阿甘诗。就像每十二年才开一次的葛林芝花(桑格姆诗歌中最重要的主题之一),甘德的"桑格姆声学"是桑格姆的共鸣和写照,在加利福尼亚的风景中,或是通过海洋、山脉、田园、森林和荒地,为我们这个时代揭示了"人类的自我体验"和"自然现象"之间的有机关联。甘德的诗展现了加利福尼亚的风景和美国方言的表达,但无论如何都不能被视为是对泰米尔桑格姆文化精神的模仿、转化或挪用。一个领域的神圣性并没有被另一个领域的神圣性所侵犯,从严格的时间角度来说,后者是一个外来的实体。就这一点而言,甘德的"桑格姆声学"甚至不能被解读为将古典泰米尔文化的语汇翻译成现代美国语汇的一种令人肃然起敬的尝试。

甘德的"桑格姆声学"需要被解读为由其不变的精神所构成的"桑格姆意识"的自由生发和深刻映照的<u>化身</u>。如果说泰米尔桑格姆以其公认的、独特的泰米尔景观特征而跃然纸上，那么"桑格姆声学"则唤起了加利福尼亚景观的脉动精神。每个时空领域的独特性在道德上都保持不变。在甘德的诗歌中，特别引人注目的是，通过每个领域的独特性，一种"普遍的桑格姆精神"得以显现，各种不同的肉身的自我、存在状态和无法比拟的景观的隐喻性联系都融合到了一起。甘德的诗歌以一种复杂而精密的方式，对东方和西方、泰米尔和英语的简单化和还原主义的二元论提出了质疑。甘德的包容性和包罗万象的眼光超越了空间和时间的等级性压迫，因此具有永恒的品质，使读者看到他的诗中人物像菩萨一样有多个化身。"桑格姆精神"的"永恒"状态在甘德的作品中似乎是一种顿悟。用神秘主义者威廉·布莱克的话来说，"桑格姆声学"通过构成其精神大厦的对立，达到了一种诗意的进步。

正是在泰米尔语和加州桑格姆的密集而丰富的融合中，所有多重或不同的回音、共鸣、声音以及各个领域的色彩都被有意识地表现出来，"声学"这个词也从而获得了清新、鲜明的意义。每种景观犀利的细微差别、微妙的音调和深沉的色彩都出色地证明了人类精神的普遍性。这种普遍性虽然与物质世界紧密相连，但却可以通过具体经验的力量而不是模糊、无定形的想法来超越时间和空间压抑的界限。对物质性真相的充分认识确实成就了具有超越性、整体性的"桑格姆生命精神"的诞生时刻。弗罗斯特·甘德的"桑格姆声学"就是一种范例。

外一篇

过往的未来：煤矿开采
——中美诗歌与环境危机

弗罗斯特·甘德

我们的采煤技术以惊人的速度不断进步：最早是暗挖机，然后是顶板锚栓支架、通风装置、机械装载、传送系统、露天开采，以及最近也就是大约三四十年前开始的 "山顶移除采矿"。仅在美国的一个州，即西弗吉尼亚州，超过 40 万英亩的森林山脉被摘顶，1200 英里的溪流在短短几年内被填埋。覆盖物（剩余的岩石）堵塞了邻近的山谷。这种挖掘方式产生的泥浆包含了大量化学废物和有毒金属。挖掘之后产生的副产品，如粉尘和有毒气体，会在发电厂煤炭燃烧的过程中被释放。

因为大多数煤炭含有黄铁矿或硫化亚铁，爆破过程中会释放出硫磺气体。二氧化硫、氧化亚氮和汞等有毒气体都会挥发到空气中。当然，二氧化碳也一样。大气中碳的同位素指数将其与化石燃料的燃烧直接联系起来。煤炭是最肮脏的化石燃料，产生的二氧化碳是天然气的两倍。我们空气中的二氧化碳，其密度的增长速度比以往任何时候都要高出 200 倍。二氧化碳能积聚反射的热量，并像枕头一样把它固定在地球的表面。同时，二氧化硫会形成酸雨从天而降；而汞则会渗入海洋。

到 21 世纪末，在煤炭首次被集中开采的短短三百年后，地下积累了三亿多年的大量的煤炭已经被燃烧释放到大气中。这两个数字之间的关系，即三百和三亿，代表了六个数量级差别。

到 2030 年，美国燃煤发电的消耗可能会每年增长 1.9%，其增速比石油和天然气的能源消耗之和还要快。美国有超过 400 家燃煤电厂，至少还有 114 家电厂正在建设中。在中国，煤炭正为前所未有的工业化发展提供动力。有科学家预测，到 2100 年煤炭将为世界提供一半的能源。之后的一百年内，地球上所有可开采的煤炭储备将被耗尽。

***

即使从写作的时间和背景中被挖掘出来，一首诗也是一种新奇的可再生能源。

***

在 21 世纪的第一个十年里，我们变得国际化了，能听到不同的声音和方言，但我们意识到，总的来说，支配世界历史的语言实践正变得越来越标准化、功利化和可转录化。我们已经成为驾驭声音片段的专家。我们在报纸、电视、八卦和闲聊中吸收各种陈词滥调和其他现成的、规范性的语言模式。有了短信、语法和拼写检查的电脑程序，我们在输入一个词或句子的过程中会有一系列的选择来帮助完成。程序生成的这些选择符合了惯例中可能性最高的选项。语言可能性的范围被压缩成高概率的词或短语。这样的捷径虽然有用，却怂恿我们进入了预先设定的固定表达模式，从而限制了思考，制约了感知。

全球化把我们集合到了一起，工业化和人口的压力给自然环境造成了极大的负面影响。动植物物种岌岌可危，将从地球上消失。我们中的有些人会想，人类能否以自己独立于其他物种的种族中心主义观点为由，而对自然资源继续大肆掠夺；从长远来看，这种态度是否会导致不可估量的损失，将其他物种以及我们自己置于险境。

我们对环境所造成的影响肯定会影响到一个诗人的写作手法和素材。但诗歌有益于生态吗？它能否显示或致力于见证人类和非人类领域间共生的经济价值？除了主题和参照以外，句法、断句或诗在页面上的排列如何能表达生态伦理？如果我们的感知经验大多是复写本式的或是无休止的并列和碎片化；如果事件鲜有谨慎的开始或结尾，而只有层次、持续时间和过渡；如果自然过程已经被人类的观察所改变并对其作出反应，那么诗歌如何能记录下这样复杂的相互依存关系，从而让我们与世界能够进行对话？

当然，东西方语言文学都有悠久的田园诗传统，即以自然景观为中心的诗歌。我自己对"自然诗"不太感兴趣，因为在这种诗里，自然只是作为主题出现。让我感兴趣的是一种所谓的"生态诗"。生态诗在主题和形式上探索了自然和文明、语言和感知之间的关系。

我不愿意提出任何特定的综合美学观点，以此来体现语言意义和实际现象的结合。堆肥，即有机物的混合，并不比严格的斐波那契数列或家蝇眼睛中 400 个面的几何对称更自然。这就取决于我们想如何对自然作出隐喻，没有任何定义是权威的。

此刻，中国和美国似乎正在进行一场拔河比赛，以确定哪个国家能释放出更多的二氧化碳。对这两个国家而言，自然资源都仅服务于短视的人类所要达到的目的。也许这些事实让这两个国家的诗人承担了特殊的责任。或许环境素养的发展——我指的是解读环境与其居民关联的能力，可以通过诗歌素养得到促进；也许诗歌素养也能通过环境素养得以深化。

诗歌不仅仅是对智性的补充，还提供了其本身所固有的、甚至是无可比拟的洞察力。诗歌的意义既不能定量，也无可验证，所以与信息和商业语言相比，能够提供别样的、更微妙深刻的表达。生态诗甚至可以阐明一种去中心化的主体经验，强调无论是自我还是世界上的事物都不能脱离包含它们的世界而存在。也许中国诗人早在几个世纪前就为这种意识开创了先例。但我对当代诗人如何改造和复制这些先例来创造出适应我们目前紧迫状况的作品尤为感兴趣。

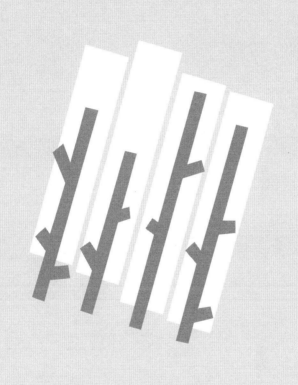

For Ashwini Bhat & Lakshmi Bhat

a garden without lichens/is a garden without hope
—*Drew Milne*

My every moment/I've lived/a second time ...
—*Giuseppe Ungaretti*
(Geoffrey Brock, trans.)

Who need be afraid of the merge?
—*Walt Whitman*

TWICE ALIVE

AN ECOLOGY OF INTIMACIES

AUTHOR'S NOTE

What many of us learned in high school about lichen—that it's an indicator species for pollution (litmus, in fact, is derived from lichens), and that it's the synergistic alliance of a fungus and algae or cyanobacteria—is largely true, but simplified. If lichen ecology has more to do with collaboration than competition, it's nevertheless true that collaboration is transformative. With lichen, which may be more related to animals than plants, the original organisms are changed utterly in their compact. They can't return to what they were. And according to Anne Pringle, one of the leading contemporary mycologists (with whom I had the lucky opportunity to collaborate), it may be that lichen do not, given sufficient nutrients, age. Anne and other contemporary biologists are saying that our sense of the inevitability of death may be determined by our mammalian orientation. Perhaps some forms of life have "theoretical immortality." Lichens can reproduce asexually, and when they do, bits of both partners are dispersed together to establish in a new habitat. How long can the partners of a lineage continue to reproduce? No one knows. The thought of two things that merge, mutually altering each other, two things that, intermingled and interactive, become one thing that does not age, brings me to think of the nature of intimacy. Isn't it often in our most intimate relations that we come to realize that our identity, all identity, is combinatory?

AUBADE

Can you hear dawn edging close, hear • soft light with its vacuum
fingertips • gripping the bedroom wall, an understated • what?
exhilaration? Can you hear the voices, • if they can be called voices,
of towhees • scratching in the garden and then • the creaky low
husky • voice flecked with sleep beside you in bed • telling a dream
slowly as though in real time, • and now, interrupting that dream,
can you • make out the voice, if it can be • called a voice, of
absence speaking • intimately to you, directly, I know • you must
hear it feelingly, a low vibration in • your bones, for don't you find
yourself • absorbed in a next moment beyond your given life?

UNTO OURSELVES

Even when we realized we'd stopped, in every
essential way stopped moving forward, when
we came to see we were descending, even
more tightly bound to the vortex
as images rushed by in front of us and a blue
whale rotted on the sand in Bolinas, its stink
drifting southward where dozens of barnacled
forty-foot grays, dead from starvation, began to hulk
against the shore, the white-tufted foreheads
of waves smashing against those
knolls of oily decomposing flesh, it was
everywhere we looked if we cared to look
out over bitesize squares of cheese
and Saintsbury wine into the hum
taking place under a coved moon, or cared to
listen to clumped wild-rye
shushing the dunes
while pulverized rock shrieked along fault lines
in decibels so muted only the soles of our feet,
conducting the ground's sound
up into our tali, could register what
was happening
right there where our lives had been
cut off from themselves and become something else
drained of substance, steeped in the privilege
against which we protested with those we called
our friends—the ones who lately seemed
to contract backward from our greetings,
giving us to suspect
that they too sensed something askew, the
skip at the center of ourselves or just an
inkling of abyssal unhappiness was it? concentrated
into the early evenings

like one of those spectral white
fallow deer introduced to the headlands
that began to outcompete
native species and so,
before they were slaughtered every one
by hired hunters, inciting
arguments about what was native if
all systems are given to change. Maybe
our ear twitches. Maybe the deer's ear
twitches. But we still can't quite
make out in the dimness
what we're looking at, can we?
Nor is there interim from the tumult of in-
coming, the masticating chores, ping-
pings begging immediate response, the sheer
overabundance of the present
shame which plugs up each minute and
stands in now for whatever it meant
to live oneself before every gesture
became performance for an audience
we imagine never to be finished
with looking at us. And as for the budding-out
of being we'd called passion? or the sensual
moments phrased into our gait
when we were coming to feel something,
when our shadows merged (not as
romance, but the real consequence
of our mutuality) with
shadows of conifers along the steep
ravine, and completely naked and
without relief, the world parsed us
into the inhuman where rosette
lichen surged across rocks lacking nothing
that might be needed to answer
for our existence?
By now, some of us,
outmaneuvered by the economy,

were lying around Dolores Park like fallen fruit
waiting to rot. Others found themselves
receptive to a trivial, self-justifying kindness.
What with coral belching up its algae, evaporating
stars, the waking tundra, how could we bear, we
wondered to each other, even the weight of
our own sorry initiatives? *Life,* someone
countered, *is pure gratuitous magnitude. Just
look: the light is there, grace itself.* But
it was already noon and as we looked,
the colors of the hills began to blanch,
and all around us, in the field of the visible,
we sensed, without speaking, duration's ebb.

TWICE ALIVE

mycobiont just beginning to **en-
wrap** photobiont, each to become
something else, its own life and a
contested mutuality, twice alive,
algal cells **swaddled** in clusters

you take a 3-lens jeweler's loupe to inspect the **holdfast**
of the umbilicate lichens then the rock-tripe lichens
then the irenic Amanita mushroom
swarming with a kind of mite that has no anus
then the delicious chanterelles called Trumpets of Death

supreme parsimony in drought
lets lichen live on
sporadic events
of dew and fog, a **velvety**
tomentum and the wet thallus

I crush oak moss between finger and thumb
for its sweet **perfume** persistent on
your skin when I touch your throat, so slow
to evaporate, the memory of seeing
sunburst lichen on the sandstone cliff

though crustose lichen relish
decay, **vagrant** lichen go all
hygroscopic, spores spurting
out through walls **split**
at the invagination fronts

but if herbivores eat **wolf** lichen they
die and if carnivores eat it they die
writhing in pain with the exception of mice
it is rarely possible to tell
if lichen is dead or alive

the fuzz of **fecal** dust from
lichenivorous mites
triggers woodcutter's eczema,
the bane of loggers knee-deep
in **sweet** fern sawing down cedar

in the presence of water, photobionts go turgid
in hours of dark respiration, a spermatic **green-corn** smell
takes the shape of a lamellated mushroom
in cavitating symplasts, spores loosen
into the **elongation** zone on a night of caterwauling loons

so evening finds us at this woods' edge where

at a dead oak's base
shoestring-rot **glimmers,** its luminescent
rhizomes reflected from the eyes
of a foraging raccoon that doesn't yet sense us

air ghostly and damp clings
as we step from our woods
to look across the field toward the first
lane of lit houses, their dull **pewter**
auras restrained by wet haze

cordyceps—the brown of your eyes softened
with rain and remotely **fluorescent**—dissolve
into **slime** after a few days, whatever we thought
we were following was following us, its
intention unlinked to our own

SANGAM ACOUSTICS

FOREST

Erogenous zones in oaks
        slung with
                stoles of lace lichen the

sun's rays spilling
        through leaves in
                broken packets a force

call it nighttime
        thrusts mushrooms up
                from their lair

of spawn mycelial
        loam the whiff of port
                they pop into un-

trammeled air with the sort of
        gasp that follows
                a fine chess move

like memories are they? or punctuation? was it
        something the earth said
                to provoke our response

tasking us to recall
        an evolutionary
                course our long ago

initiation into
        the one-
            among-others

and within
        my newborn noticing have you
            popped up beside me love

or were you here from the start
        a swarm of meaning and decay
            still gripping the underworld

both of us half-buried holding fast
        if briefly to a swelling
            vastness while our coupling begins

to register in the already
        awake compendium that offers
            to take us in you take me in

and abundance floods us floats
        us out we fill each
            with the other all morning

breaks as birdsong over us
        who rise to the surface
            so our faces might be sprung

Aroused by her inaccessibility, he aches for more
of her life to live inside him. Watching

                  the breakers, standing so close he can feel
                     heat coming off her wet scalp. What is

his relation to this person
before him, so familiar and foreign? The way

                he searches out her face, he searches out himself. Gusts
                    thrash crests of swell, spring grasses twirl

circles in the sand where they stand without speaking. She
wants him to know it's all charged, even grass

                 positive, pollen negative, so when grass waves,
           it sweeps the air for pollen. He feels electricity all around

as though the wild drama of the coming storm were already
aware of them, foreigners on this shore. Little

                  sapphire-blue flowers speckle the dunes.
                He wonders if he has let himself flatten out

into a depthless sheet, like escalator stairs, whether in the end
he'll disappear underground without the smallest lurch

of resistance. But when her lavish face turns toward him
beaming, the corners of her eyes wind-wet,

he yields to that excess, he reappears to himself.

IN THE MOUNTAINS

"No hay exterior del cuerpo. O mejor dicho,
el exterior ocurre dentro del cuerpo"
—Juan Sebastián Cárdenas

If the April dog days reach her before your note does

If at your back door, a mushroom speckled with roving mites
turns the color of rodent teeth

Then her thighs will tremble, her head go light as she tries to stand

If her irises flare, if your collied face stares back from her pupils dull
as a writ

Then you must acknowledge the presentiment that you've been
cored

If you take another sip of dust, trying to remember what to say

If the sludge she calls your sadness stops damming-up your veins

Could she glimpse what was there before you turned inside yourself?

If the regrets edge up behind you chattering

Then she will blindfold you saying: taste this

If it takes just one more crossed-out name to complete the bitterness

If ululations rising from the hills are answered in her face

Then whatever you gasp while she lies over you will sound like
nonsense from a play

If you reflexively choose the first response that precludes thinking

Then she will cry out *Oh no* as though surprised she can't stop it

If the Western Ghats swallow a carbonized sun

If she mistakes that tic at your eye's crease for a signal

If when she sets her basket on the counter, the ripest mango topples
   from the peak

You must forget the other hands that have opened her robe

If local animals make themselves nocturnal to avoid you, if swarms
of laughing thrushes no longer descend from the summit

Then the barest gleam from her eyes in the night will reel you in

But if this orange lichen—gossiping across boulders—blackens,
   curls, and goes silent?

PASTORAL

The rain broke off   an hour earlier, the turn
the turn-signal indicator ceased   the last of its clucking, and

we arrived   at the abandoned farm arrived
with others just now   bailing themselves out

from their cars, our voices   pitched in some ad-
mixture of ease and   exhilaration, some

adventure in happiness if   there were such a thing and it wasn't
pretend: laughing, slamming   the doors, we were miscible, we believed

we were friends, remember that?   and your floriferous
bridesmaids still wearing those   purple plumeria headbands

like Goa hippies. The serpentine   footpath to the river steamed—
it steamed in sunlight   adding to the fullness without

adding weight. You,   to whom this place was a given,
sacred even, and so not given   *to* you, pointed out

peacock tracks in the mud. Through   an old orchard on either side
of us, where swollen jackfruit   hung on slender limbs,

swarms of midges   bobbed up and down
like balled hairnets in the light   breeze. Before it

became visible, we heard   the river *river*
and behind it the   gurgling of runoff

down bluffs of packed alluvium.   Jacaranda perfume
mixed with pong   from your neighbor's

breeder-houses. Who could look   into that afternoon and see
it closing? Our whole   queue halted when you went

to one knee, when you crouched   at a puddle to coo
to a fat toad. Gone   quiet, we were hypnotized

by the signature   enthusiasm
in your face. As the sun   cleared the clouds, you

glanced back to find my eyes   eyes fixed on you, and what
I felt then   gave me cause

to recall   the pleasure breaking out
on the faces of musicians   in that pause

between their last note between   their last note and
the applause. What   you said, what I said. What

we did we did until there was no interval between us.

WASTELAND (FOR SANTA ROSA)

Green spring grass on
the hills had cured
by June and by July

gone wooly and
brown, it crackled
underfoot, desiccated while

within the clamor of live
oaks, an infestation of
tiny larvae clung

to the underleaves,
feeding between
veins. Their frass, that

fine dandruff of excrement
and boring dust, tinkled
as it dropped onto dead leaves

below the limbs. You
could hear it twenty
feet away, tinkling.

Across the valley, on
　　　　Sugarloaf Ridge, the full
　　　　　　　moon showed up

　　　　　　　　　　like a girl doing cartwheels.
　　　　　　　No one goes on living
　　　　　　the life that isn't there.

Below a vast column of
　　　　smoke, heat, flame, and
　　　　　　wind, I rose, swaying

　　　　　　　　　and tottering on my
　　　　　　　erratic vortex, extemporizing
　　　　　my own extreme weather, sucking up

acres of scorched
　　　topsoil and spinning it
　　　　　　outward in a burning sleet

　　　　　　　　of filth and embers that
　　　　　　catapulted me forward
　　　　　with my mouth open

in every direction at once. So

I came for you, churning, turning
the present into purgatory

because I need to turn
everything to tragedy before
I can see it, because

it must be
leavened with remorse
for the feeling to rise.

AUBADE II
for Ötzi

Pulling the arrow's shaft • from his own shoulder • on the east
ridge with • and an axe of solid copper and • ibex meat undi-
gested • conifer pollen, so late spring • bearskin snowshoes • a
pouch with his firelighting kit • flint flakes and a tinder conk • the
mushroom kindling an ember for hours • after he turned onto
his stomach • froze & thawed & froze again • for 5,000 years •
what beyond pain • did he hear as the light flickered • flickered
on the mountain's face • what entered his body through the ears •
through the desolate desolated desolation of his eyes • what did he
take • for which he had no name

UNTO OURSELVES II:
THE PERSISTENCE OF DISPERSED WORLDS

Firs trembled at the edge of a massive debris flow

in the asphalt-heat of summer

just between you and me, said the field guide

in an undertone leaning forward, you have to

get beyond the expectation that you're

ever going to pull things together

it was a queer thing to say in a queer time

we use a gender-neutral pronoun we said

to which she answered Whoever

thought anyone was just one thing?

when we got back my friends were jumpy

Did you see the quindes?

Did you see the tucusitos?

The picaflores, the chupamirtos—are they over there?

Across the wall?

What of the huichichiquis?

Don't tell me you blinked as it hovered face to your face

fanning you with the mill of its wings, the guide said

no b.s. did you see the huitzillo?

we admitted we'd witnessed the chuparosa in Petaluma

a large blue-throated one up from Mexico

but the tzunún fled too soon

as if it knew what we would do to its garden

where sheathed filaments of cyanobacteria

wakened by winter rains were serpentining through the soil

leaving long sticky trails through the evening

while we stood on our porch and admired

the soft edges of things in moonlight as though

we were in a Gerhard Richter painting or some seductive

image from an advertising campaign

developing in a bath of chemicals

how to recover the play of life itself yes

the yes of course yes we now yes!

we tried walking in someone else's shoes

but fuck that really it was a sham,

like frogs HAZMAT trucks were beeping as they

reached their destination down the block

though who could take notice

with their eyes glued to the new pilot

the reporter didn't say *fire tomato* he said

fire tornado the abyss with one eye

was there only inconsequential difference

between *I contain multitudes* and *be sure*

to like us or those other hortatory sops

we told each other to make the unbearable bearable?

our extrafloral nectaries were still attracting insects

despite we'd sprayed them with Roundup

the spidery bass player kept to his corner of the stage

as one world is bound to another by silence

and catfacing always infects the blossom-side

in the middle of the argument we noticed

we confront each other like two regions of warped space

swallowing the gravitational screams

emitted from our merging holes

and though we admit to a certain amount of preening and swanking

each assumes our own is the meat-forward dish

You're kidding, I overheard the guide say, really? That's

what you did with your life? So

the lonely night was adjourned like a can of green paint

splashed onto the dining car's windows as we watched

lengths of border wall rush past and go by

the conductor's recorded voice said Make use of thy salt hours

for already thou art deep within the affliction

TWICE ALIVE II: TAHOE NATIONAL FOREST

if that's a mass of black jelly fungi
on the rotting pine branch, if that's a thumb-long
translucent egg sac **pulsating** behind the termite queen
if the rising sun through the blinds wakes us together or
will tomorrow, if **witch's butter** could learn to speak

long soft sarongs of **moss**
ensorcel rocks treestumps up-
lifts of granite and gneiss
pine needles blackberry brambles
arching up wet and **tousled**

as we descend a scrub hillside
our breath visible in flighty morning
air, we enter the forest of quaking
aspen, **spongy** ground
on either side of the path riffled
by creamy edible morels and

poisonous **false** morels, song
of moss under our breath, before you left
you said *Don't be so rational, electronics*
are rational and I wondered what change
I might make that my next words **not** be so

then your telegram of tiny black mosquitoes kept me awake
all night on the porch I could hear big **moths**
before I saw them, when finally I laid down in the huge space
your **absence** left me, the cat pawed my chest
while your towel with its sour smell muffled my face

while I'm dogged through the day by quick sniffs of
sickness, the **sorghum**-thick snot insists
I too am a fleshy protuberance risen momently
from some tangled mycelium so the dead also
speak when I speak **oh** holy holy communion

then the getting **tired** happened
then the white-flecked brown pigeon
flattened itself into the sand, some force
expresses us before we can name it
fragrance **whelms** from incense-cedars

SANGAM ACOUSTICS II

POST-FIRE FOREST

Shadows of shadows without canopy,
phalanxes of carbonized trunks and
snags, their inner momentum shorted-out.
They surround us in early morning
like plutonic pillars, like mute clairvoyants
leading a Sursum Corda, like the excrescence
of some long slaughter. All that moves
is mist lifting, too indistinct to be called
ghostly, from scorched filamental
layers of rain-moistened earth. What
remains of the forest takes place
in the exclamatory mode. Cindered
utterances in a tongue from which
everything trivial has been volatilized,
everything trivial to fire. In a notch,
between near hills stubbled
with black paroxysm, we spot
a familiar sun, liquid glass globed
at the blowpipe's tip. If this landscape
is dreaming, it must dream itself awake.

You have, everyone notes, a rare talent
for happiness. I wonder how
to value that, walking through wreckage.
On the second day, a black-backed
woodpecker answers your call, but we
search until twilight without finding it.

Maybe enough light • to score a wave • reflecting moonlight, sand • reflecting moonlight and you • spotting from shore • what you see only • as silhouette against detonating bands • of blue-white effervescence • when the crown of the falling • swell explodes upward • as the underwave blows through it • a flash of visibility quickly • snuffed by night • the surf fizzling and churning • remitting itself to darkness • with a violent stertor • in competition with no other sounds

paddling through dicey backwash • the break zone of • waist-high NW swell • as into a wall of obsidian • indistinguishable from night sky • diving under, paddling fast • and before I sit • one arm over my board • I duck and • listen a moment underwater • to the alien soundscape • not daytime's clicks and whines of • ship engines and sonar • but a low-spectrum hum • the acoustic signature of fish, squid, • crustaceans rising en masse • to feed at the surface I feel • an eerie peacefulness veined with fear

after twenty minutes the eyes • adjust, behind the hand dragging through water • bioluminescent trails • not enough light • to spot boils • or flaws in nearing • waves appear even larger • closing-in fast • then five short strokes into a dimensionless • peeler, two S-shaped turns, the • kick out, and from shore • your shout

it is cowardice that turns my eyes • from the now-empty beach • for with you I became • aware of an exceptional chance • I don't believe in • objective description, only • this mess, experience, the perceived • world sometimes shared • in which life doesn't • endure, only • the void endures • but your vitality stirred it • leaving trails of excitation • I've risen from the bottom of • myself to find

• I exist in you • exist in me and • against odds I've known even rapture, • rare event, • which calls for • but one witness

IN THE MOUNTAINS, PLACER COUNTY

...whose blunt finger, its hornblende-nail clipped,
circles (so lightly across the crevice knob)

And her green delight of serpentine
laughter (as their tram swoops) over the trunk valley

Car door slammed behind her, she faces the cirque
in denim cutoffs (risen to her pudendum)

And sees no gap in the pleasures nestled
in his eyes watching (her eyes watching)

Above the mission of his face, they swing like
church bells (for mass always sways outward)

A taste of jaggery and warm pennies (oh no,
oh no!) in a wet score grooved by glacial erratics

Where, he asks, as she initiates the uplift, and when
did you learn to do that? (decamping downslope)

A rattler riding its coil (her torso on her hips), she leaves
chatter marks on a succession of moraines

(Dark paired suns) the aureoles dilate
as suction-eddies whirligig along the melt stream

When the supplicant slowly bends, long
thighs separate along the joint plane

No undertow of doubt, every part willing, the forest
encroaches ashen earth (when her knees begin to jerk)

PASTORAL

Together,
you
standing
before me before
the picture
window, my arms
around you, our
eyes pitched
beyond our
reflections into—

("into" I'd
written, as
though *there*
swung at the end
of a tunnel,
a passage dotted
with endless
points of
arrival, as
though our gaze
started just outside
our faces and
corkscrewed its way
toward the horizon,
processural,
as if looking
took time to happen
and weren't
instantaneous,
offered whole in
one gesture
before we

ask, before our
will, as if the far
Sonoma mountains
weren't equally ready
to be beheld as
the dead
fly on the sill)—

the distance, a
broad hill of
bright mustard flowers
the morning light
coaxes open.

WASTELAND

You will forever regret the petty-righteous cruelties
you acted out on her,

                              the neem tree without blossoms, the twig girdler,
                                                          the burying

beetle, a yellow-and-black apple borer with
its disgusting stench

                              which decimated the garden while you were
                                                          distracted. Right

when she was leading you out of something.
A laceration inside a laceration

                              into which you tugged her back each night
                                                          until nothing was left

between you but a fear of aging and
your unwearying

                              self-concern. That night, the last night
                                                          before

your so-called return, she sent
you a note.

Baby, I miss you, imagine

you're sitting in your leather swivel chair

with your silk boxers on, I'll lift my dress a little

and sit on you (you won't have trouble

sliding into me), my back to you, your hands

inside my sleeves

Look up and the horizon line has gone
                    red as a transparent artery while below you
an alligator-lizard continues to
                    slide down the warm ash of the
Long Valley Caldera to dig out
                    her nest in toxic fumes. The years
of your footsteps have chewed
                    a worn path into lichen spotting
tuff around the rim. You've lost
                    your cadence. No one needs
to tell you that. Her absence
                    goes through and through
you like a winze through
                    crumbling bedrock. No-
thing remains in session
                    but the congress of ants.

AUBADE III

We were servicing the pools of the wealthy • we were opening the
passenger door for the dog • the dog who waits in the truck • dog
staring at the restaurant entrance • so when we come out again
with a napkin • wrapped around a chunk of burrito • whimpers
with excitement • and we don't • feel entirely alone • though it's
true • Yo, la peor de todas • at Arion the printers • were dampen-
ing linen • so the type would cast a shadow • before they tossed
slugs of type • back into the hellbox • in the evening • we tried
to cure a phantom • limb with a mirror • but what is missing • is
inside us. A few were • throwing gang signs and smoking Reggie
• before we boarded at pre-dawn • to sit forever on the runway •
sucking up the spent fuel • of the plane before us • the overhead
ducts spewing noxious air • reflected in the dark window • our
own eyes looking back • looking blank • while neutrinos sleet
through us

UNTO OURSELVES III: TO SEE WHAT'S THERE

To see what's there and not already
patterned by familiarity—for an unpredicted
whole is there, casting a pair of shadows, manipulating
its material, advancing, assembling enough
kinship that we call it *life,* our life, what
is already many lives, the dimensions of
its magnitude veiled to us as we live it—

Across the cytoplasm of adjacent cells
goes a signal that turns you toward me, turns
me into you. We are coupled in quiet
tumult, convergent arguments, an alien
rhythm becoming familiar. A rhythm
of *I am here, never to be peeled away.*
We are become one thing
                                        listening

for what's there and not. Through the storm,
neem trees on the hill stamp wildly
in their roots. We have passed through
the spring, but what thing has passed
through us? Now your laughter
transparentizes me. And whose sense
of the self doesn't swerve? Your unconditional
foreignness grows conditional, stops
being foreign at all. With your nearness,
my lens on the world shifts. A peristaltic
contraction courses through us as a single
wave. No longer can we keep our distance.
Our lips brush, or the tips of ourselves.

But what language are you whispering to me,
your teeth stained by Nilgiri tea, above the trills
and whistles in the high limbs, above the screech
of a bulldozer blade shoving rubble
up the wounded street, above the silence
of an eyeless tick climbing a grass stem? I understand
nothing but the lust your voice incites, the
declamatory tenderness. How, and who can say
what force has cued up this hour for our
small voices to merge into a carnality
that did not exist before now?

Having come to this unforeseen
conjunction, we slip
into one another, we take hold
in a pulse of heat, in a yes and no,
for already we can see
we are no longer what we were

as I find you within me—not fused, not
bonded, but nested. And for you, is it
the same?—the intensity of such
investment, each of us excited
by the volatility of the other which
propels us in a rush as something—
perhaps our lips brush or
the tips of ourselves—strips
away what?—what was before? Was there
even anything before?

The reconfiguration is instantaneous
experience. It is *being*
itself. But whose being now? Was I
endowed with some special pliability so

that becoming part of you I didn't pass
through my own nihilation? And what
does the death of who-you-were mean to me
except that now you are present, constantly.

Because excess is what it took
for us to transform, to effulge. You cast
your life beyond itself. Can't you sense me
within your ecstatic openness
like rain mingling with red earth?
Without you I survived and with you
I live again in a radical augmentation
of identity because we have
effaced our outer limits, because
we summoned each other. In you,
I cast my life beyond itself.

TWICE ALIVE III:
CIRCUMAMBULATION OF MT. TAMALPAIS

maculas of light fallen weightless from
pores in the canopy our senses
part of the **wheeling** life around us and through
an undergrowth stoked with **the unseen**
go the reverberations of our steps

as we hike upward mist holds
the **butterscotch** taste of Jeffrey pine
to the air until we reach a serpentine
barren, **redbud** lilac and open sky, a crust
of frost on low-lying clumps of manzanita

at Redwood Creek, two
tandem runners cross
a wooden bridge over
the stream ahead of us the raspy
check check check of a **scrub jay**

hewing to the Dipsea path while
a plane's slow groan diminishes bayward,
my sweat-wet shirt going cool
around my torso as another runner
goes by, his **cocked** arms held too high

Cardiac Hill's granite boulders appear
freshly sheared Look, you say,
I can see the Farallon Islands there
to the south over those long-backed hills
one behind another a crow **honks**

the moon still up over Douglas
firs on the climb to Rock Spring yellow-
jackets and Painted Lady butterflies
settle on the path where some underground trickle moistens the soil

I predict you'll keep to the shade of
the laurels to **nibble** your
three-anchovy-slices-over-cheese
sandwich while I sprawl on a boulder
in full **sun** sucking a pear

the frass of caterpillars tinkles onto beds of dry
leaves under the oak where a hawk **alights**
with its retinue of **raging** crows we are prey to the ache
of not knowing what will be revealed as
the world lunges forward to introduce itself

clusters of tiny green dots, **bitter** oyster,

line the black stick held in your hand, weak
trees leaning into us as if we were part
of the **wet dark** that sustains their roots
under dead leaves and that Armillaria

since honey mushrooms suck from
the soil chemicals that trigger a tree's
defences, they leech the tree's sap
undetected all the while secreting toxins
to stave off competing species

but in the inseparable
genetic **mosaic** of their thin
root filaments the identity
of any singular species blurs among interactive populations, **twice** alive

near the summit, a gleaming
slickenside outcrop
sanctifies the path winding
through a precinct of **greenschists**
whose **lethal** minerals sterilize the ground

the hum of some large insect
Immelmanning around

our heads calls to mind,
you tell me, the **low drone**
of a Buddhist chant

but now we really hear chanting
we can't decode—*Don't
be so rational*—a congregate speech
from the **redtrembling** sprigs, a
vascular language prior to our

breathed language, corporeal, chemical,
drawing our sound into its harmonic, tuning
us to what we've not yet seen, the surround
calling us, theory-less, toward an inference
of horizontal connections there at

ground level, an incantation in-
dependent (of us) but detectable, **consummate**
always resistant (to us) but inciting
our recognition of what it might mean
to be **here**—among others human and not—

here, home, where ours is another of the small
voices taking us over, over ourselves
over into the **nothing-between**, the out

of sight of ourselves, a litany from
spore-bearing mouths as

hyphae stretch their **long** necks
and open their throats opening
a link between systems
a supersaturation of syntax
an **arousal** even as slow-

rolling walls of high-decibel
sonar blow out the **ears** of whales and
fires burn uncontrolled and
slurry pits leak into the creek, etc.
etc., femicides, war, righteous

insistence and still
and **still** the lived sensation fits
into the living sensorium, can't
you hear—*Don't be so rational*—
the world **inhale?**—hear

the call from elsewhere which
is just where we are, no, even
closer, **inside** us inside the blood-
pulse of our bodies, the bristle of
our mosses, the **embrace**—, and exhale

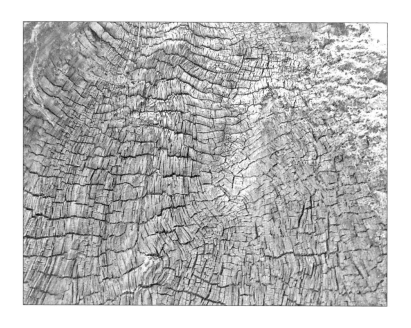

THE REDWOODS

• • •

—while nearby, but where?

／ ＼

in that terpenated air among   iterated redwood limbs

＼   ／ ＼

now flocked   with mats of epiphyte,

／ |

／   a Steller's jay starts and restarts

／   ／

its shredded arpeggios—   *not description*—and

＼   ＼

one of a nesting murrelet's soft   black eyes mirrors

                    /
the harlequinades of a vole,   plump, whiskered
        \ |
    cylinder of fur diligently—*this is*   *not description but an un-*
            \   /
        acknowledged chapter—   stuffing its cheeks
            /
    with green needles

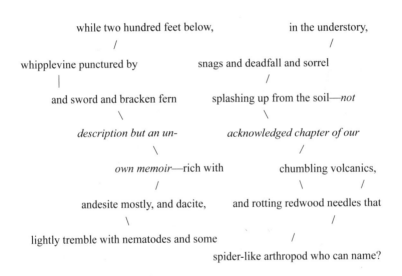

while two hundred feet below,   in the understory,
            /   /
whipplevine punctured by   snags and deadfall and sorrel
            | /
    and sword and bracken fern   splashing up from the soil—*not*
                \   \
        description but an un-   *acknowledged chapter of our*
                    \   /
            own memoir—rich with   chumbling volcanics,
                    /   \   /
        andesite mostly, and dacite,   and rotting redwood needles that
                    \   /
lightly tremble with nematodes and some   /
                                            spider-like arthropod who can name?

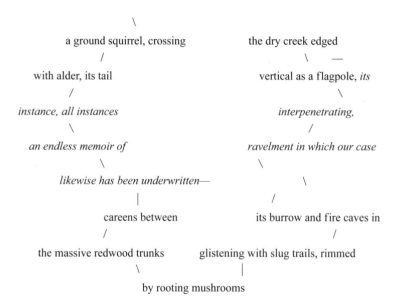

\
a ground squirrel, crossing   the dry creek edged
/   \   —
with alder, its tail   vertical as a flagpole, *its*
/   \
instance, all instances   *interpenetrating,*
\   /
an endless memoir of   *ravelment in which our case*
\   \
likewise has been underwritten—   \
| /
careens between   its burrow and fire caves in
/   /
the massive redwood trunks   glistening with slug trails, rimmed
\ |
by rooting mushrooms

REXROTH'S CABIN

On the way to • to the site of his • cabin, his temple • refurbished
from the plundered • temple of another religion • a religion of
fishermen • on the Tokelalume aka • Lagunitas Creek in Devil's
• Gulch, the path into the forest flagged • flagged on either side
with orange • sticky monkey flowers • innumerable stubby,
macho • fence lizards rush in bursts • ahead of you like heralds
as • you come up the trail, but • half a mile in, a single • Western
skink, its neon-blue tail hauled upright behind it • races diagonally
crosstrail and disappears • beneath thimbleberry brambles mantled
• with shredded spiderweb

in the epic literature of India • which all those years ago • he was
reading, lying • on this greywacke slab • above the ebulliently
plashing • creek, his head in shade, his • lanky body warm • legs
crossed in the sun's • maple light breaking through • tree limbs
pajamaed in moss • and stretching awkwardly out • out over the
gulch • from a steep hillside held in place • only by radial green
explosions • of bracken, Maidenhair fern, and • a pair of red-
spiked black caterpillars • which crawl onto his leather boots • set
side by side in the rampant pipevine the • caterpillars have been
devouring • in all that epic literature of India • no more than three
colors • are mentioned

See? He is here and not here. Not • unlike you yourself. Or the
water • striders in the creek • rowing in punctuated contractions •
against the drift. What • you see in the clear absolute of the water
• as you stand on some paleostump at the bank • under an electric
insect whine • distributed perfectly throughout the canopy, • what
you see below • in the pellucid water is a cluster of • six Gothic
black shadowdots • cast onto the streambed • below the thin, sand-
colored • bodies of the actual water striders • who are bowed all

but invisibly above • the tensile surface of the stream

Not here. And here. And though you • you have hiked the dirt
path through the forest • as he did before you were born • to the
familiar place, the confluence • of two modest falls, to the ground
truth • the little clearing where he snored • and fried two eggs for
breakfast and sat • cross-legged on a slab of rock scribbling • into
the future that holds you in it, • you are only still arriving • still
• arriving • no trace of the cabin left, and yet • his presence
is not • decomposable, your mind • merges with what is not • your
mind, your happiness • is radiant and you squat, listening • in the
tangible density of what is and isn't there • as you become your •
shadow fluidly contiguous • with the shadows of trees

SANGAM ACOUSTICS:
CONFLUENCE OF TIME, SPACE,
AND THE HUMAN SELF

BY N. MANU CHAKRAVARTHY[1]

Forest, Pastoral, Sea, Mountain, Wasteland. The five primary landscapes of Sangam literature are also the definitive landscapes of California, my birthplace and home. My "Sangam Acoustics" are influenced by my own experiences in India and California and by translations of Sangam poems which allude to one of those five topographies. Because cultural influences are complicated matters, even when the original is to be celebrated, and because Sangam poetics are so little known in the United States, I've asked the literary scholar N. Manu Chakravarthy to provide some context for Sangam poetics.—F. G.

"Sangam" refers to a gathering of individuals united in spirit, sharing a common vision, and, in a metaphysical sense, seeking meaning and purpose in a state of togetherness. The element of conviviality guides and nourishes the community of seekers, though it needs to be stated without any ambiguity that the commonness of seeking does not erase differences and divergences among individuals who form such a community. Homogeneity and hierarchy are alien to a true Sangam. The particular and specific visions of different individuals only enhance the spirit of Sangam.

The expression Sangam is rooted in the Jaina and Buddhist religious/ philosophical traditions, the essence of which is captured in the Buddhist prayer, "Buddham Sharanam Gacchami, Sangam Sharanam Gacchami, Dhammam Sharanam Gacchami"—meaning "I shall go to invoke the Buddha, embrace the Sangha, and follow the Dhamma." The prayer is indeed a declaration that one seeks the Buddha through the "sangha" and by adhering to the principles of the "Dhamma." The attainment of what is sought is deeply personal and, in a

---

1 N. Manu Chakravarthy, the distinguished literary critic and winner of the National Film Award for Best Critic of the Year, is Professor of English at NMKRV College, Bengaluru. He has written extensively on literature, music, feminism, politics, and cinema.

qualified sense, collective.

Classical Tamil literature has been recognized as "Sangam literature" and is acknowledged to have flourished between 300 B.C. and 300 A.D. Many claims have been advanced about the duration of the Sangam period, some so exaggerated they border on being mythological narratives. However, the term Sangam seems to have come to classical Tamil literature from Jaina and Buddhist sources.

Scholars recognize three Sangam periods and admit that texts belonging to the first Sangam do not appear to have survived. A text of grammar and rhetoric called "Tolkappiyam" is said to belong to the second Sangam, and the third Sangam comprises a wide range of lyrics on love that form an anthology called the "Kuruntokai." In accordance with thematic patterns, Tamil poems have been categorized as "Akam" and "Puram."

"Akam" poems are focused on an *inner realm*, while the "puram" ones refer to public spaces. Akam poems are essentially love poems and deal with the different existential/emotional states of the persona, whereas Puram poems are concerned with war, the glory of kings and heroes, and ethical values. Puram poetry has a historical/social context and is quite strongly grounded in the physical realities of the world. Akam poems are not, in the strict sense of the term, historical and are not realistic in a definable manner, which, however, does not mean that they have no sense of reality. Akam poetry is about the manner in which the realities of the world—and the elements of Nature—come fully alive in the experiential states of the persona/personae of the poems. Nature—through flowers, mountains, birds, animals, barren lands, forests, seasons—corresponds with the "inner landscape" of the individual. Consequently, birds, beasts, and the elemental forces of nature are consciously shifted to "alien locations" far beyond their original habitat, registering and underlining the shifting moods of the persona. The translocation/dislocation of "the natural order of things" is quite unique to Sangam poetry. In other words, the "exterior" precisely relates to the one who beholds it—through varied emotions created by states of longing, craving, union, fulfillment, separation, infidelity, betrayal, and so on. Thus, "nature" is what the human mind makes of it. It is because of this that the specific identity of a natural object dramatically alters to register an altogether different identity and essence of experience related to the emotional state of the persona. The extraordinary crisscrossing of natural elements is a great marker of the strength of the *inner landscape* that human consciousness carries, transforming external nature to match its own form and temper. Furthermore, nature exists in its various forms with all basic qualities intact, but in Sangam poetry "nature" extends beyond itself to "become" a metaphor of the mind. The metamorphosis of nature in Sangam poetry is essentially an internalization of the *exterior landscape*, dissolving distinctions of opposition and separation between the self 's intensity of experience and the so-called impassive spirit of physical reality. "Nature" is congruent with the human spirit.

Forrest Gander's "Sangam Acoustics" is, in the most exalted sense, the blossoming of the Sangam consciousness. Gander's poetry belongs to the Akam genre. Like the kurinchi flower (one of the most significant motifs of Sangam poetry) that blooms once in twelve years, Gander's "Sangam Acoustics" is Sangam resonating and illumining, in the Californian landscape, through Sea, Mountain, Pastoral, Forest, and Wasteland, revealing for our times the organic relationship between the "experiencing human self " and the "phenomena of nature." Gander's poems unfold the Californian landscape and find expression in American dialect, but they cannot, by any stretch of imagination, be regarded as imitations, cultural incorporations or appropriations of the cultural ethos of Tamil Sangam. There is no act of transgression or violation of the sanctity of one realm by another, which in strict temporal terms is an alien entity. For that matter Gander's "Sangam Acoustics" cannot even be interpreted as an inspired attempt to *translate* the cultural idiom of classical Tamil into the modern American idiom.

Gander's "Sangam Acoustics" needs to be read as a spontaneous and deeply reflective *incarnation* of the "Sangam consciousness," constituted by its immutable spirit. If Tamil Sangam comes alive with its very well-defined and unique features of Tamil landscapes, "Sangam Acoustics" evokes the pulsating spirit of the Californian landscape. The uniqueness of each spatiotemporal realm is kept ethically intact. What is strikingly fascinating in Gander's poetry is that through the uniqueness of each realm, a "universal Sangam spirit" emerges, unfolding the metaphorical confluence of varied and diverse physical selves, states of being, and apparently incomparable landscapes. In a complex and sophisticated manner, Gander's poetry contests simplistic and reductionist binaries of East and West, Tamil and English. Gander's inclusive and all-encompassing visions, transcending oppressive hierarchies of space and time, have a timeless quality, moving the reader to see the personae of his poems having several incarnations, like the Bodhisattvas. The "timeless" state of the "Sangam spirit" seems to manifest itself like an epiphany in Gander's work. Invoking the mystic William Blake, it could be said that "Sangam Acoustics" attains a poetic progression through the contraries that constitute its edifice.

It is in the dense and rich confluence of Tamil and Californian Sangam, with all the multiple and divergent echoes, resonances, sounds, colors of each realm so consciously consecrated, that the word "acoustics" gathers new and fresh meaning. The sharp nuances, the subtle tones, and the deep colors of each landscape work to brilliantly uphold the universality of the human spirit that— though strongly bound to its physical world—strives to transcend crippling boundaries of time and space through the strength of concrete experiences and not through vague and amorphous ideas. The full recognition of the truth of physicality is indeed the moment of birth of a transcendental holistic "Sangam life spirit." Forrest Gander's "Sangam Acoustics" illustrates this in an exemplary way.

ACKNOWLEDGMENTS

I'm particularly grateful, for a number of reasons, to Lynn Keller. It was she who invited me to collaborate with her, with the mycologist Anne Pringle, and with the artist Emily Arthur at Huron Mountain Wildlife Foundation, an experience that birthed the "Twice Alive" series.

And to Karin Gander, all our lives together.

Thanks to my international poet-companions among the lichens: foremost, to Brenda Hillman. Also to Mats Söderlund, Julio de la Vega, Camillo Sbarbaro, Drew Milne, Devin Johnston, Whit Griffin, and Peter O'Leary, and to Lew Welch, who wrote of lichen: "These are the stamps on the final envelope." To Paul Stamets, Lynn Margulis, Anne Pringle, David Griffiths, Thomas H. Nash, and Jane Bennett.

And to New Directions, all souls there, but especially Declan Spring, Mieke Chew, and Brittany Dennison, who were so involved with this book. And to you Eliot "El Faro" Weinberger, Calvin Bedient, James Byrne, Arthur Sze, Don Mee Choi, Roberto Harrison, Cole Swensen, Robert Hass, Sharon Olds, Nancy Kuhl, Joan Retallack, John Keene, Laura Mullen, Richard Deming, Dan Beachy-Quick, Roberto Tejada, Monica de la Torre.

Brecht, without you, without C, not a lick of this, nothing at all.

"Twice Alive" is for Lynn Keller. "Twice Alive II" is for Brenda Hillman. "Post-fire Forest" is for Maya Khosla; "The Redwoods" is for my Aussie friend Stuart Cooke from whom I purloined the form. "Sea: Night Surfing in Bolinas" is for Stephen Ratcliffe.

Photographs in "The Redwoods" are by Forrest Gander.

Thanks to the editors of the magazines that published some of these poems:

"The Redwoods" was commissioned and published by *Emergence Magazine* as a collaboration with the artist Katie Holten (eds. Bethany Ritz and Emmanuel Vaughan-Lee).

"The Redwoods" appeared with my photographs in *Lana Turner: A Journal of Arts & Criticism* (ed. Calvin Bedient).

"Forest" appeared in *Scientific American* (ed. Dava Sobel).

"Rexroth's Cabin" appeared in *Conjunctions* (ed. Bradford Morrow).

"Immigrant Sea" and "Post-fire Forest" appeared in *Forfatternes klimaaksjon*, a Norwegian climate magazine (ed. Mats Söderlund).

"Immigrant Sea" appeared in Polish translation in *Przekrój* (ed. Julia Fiedorczuk).

Poetry videos of "Immigrant Sea" and "Forest" (as "Interior Landscape") appeared at *Big Other* (ed. John Madera).

"Pastoral" appeared in *Poetry Daily* (ed. Jane Hirshfield).

"In the Mountains" appeared in *Cordite* (ed. Jeet Thayil).

Sections of "Twice Alive" appeared in *Republic of Apples, Democracy of Oranges: New Eco-Poetry from China and the U.S.* (eds. Frank Stewart, Tony Barnstone, and Ming Di, University of Hawaii Press, 2019). Thanks to Ming Di.

"Aubade" appeared in *Together in a Sudden Strangeness: America's Poets Respond to the Pandemic* (ed. Alice Quinn, Alfred A. Knopf, 2020).

I'm grateful for translations and exegesis of Sangam literature by M. L. Thangappa, A. R. Venkatachalapathy, A. K. Ramanujan, and others, and for a fruitful friendship with N. Manu Chakravarthy.